I, sailor

•••

Yo, marinero

Maria Espluga

me+mi publishing, inc.

I want to be a sailor
like my father and grandfather.

Yo quiero ser marinero
como mi padre y mi abuelo.

I rise with the sun to follow my dream.

Salgo con el sol rumbo a mi sueño.

At the horizon,
the dolphins bid me farewell.

Los delfines me acompañan hasta
el horizonte para decirme adiós.

The clouds over the endless
ocean are so beautiful!

¡Qué bonitas son las nubes
sobre el océano inmenso!

I brave the storm like a fearless pirate...

Cruzo la tormenta sin miedo, valiente como un pirata...

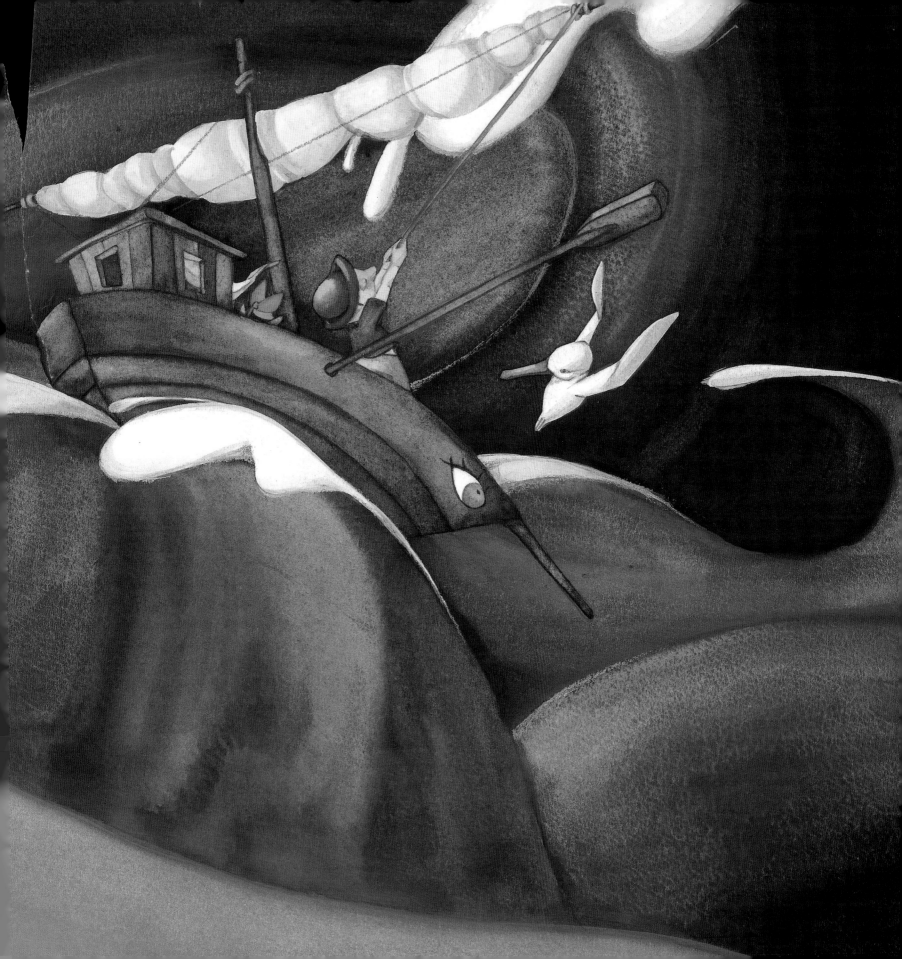

and when it's over, I rest in its tranquil embrace.

y reposo donde la calma me balancea como la abuela.

At night, when I'm homesick,
I find comfort in the Great Bear.

Me abraza la Osa del cielo
cuando de noche añoro mi cama.

In the morning I explore the depths of the crystalline sea
where dreams sleep...

De mañana fondeo el mar de cristal
donde duermen los sueños...

and I tame the Great White Whale.

y amanso la Gran Ballena Blanca.

I have gathered gifts from my adventure,
but my greatest treasure...

Me llevo un buen regalo del mar,
pero mi mayor tesoro...

is a hug from you!

¡un fuerte abrazo!

For Xavi.

me+mi publishing, inc.
400 South Knoll Street, Suite B • Wheaton, Illinois 60187

Visit us on the web at www.memima.com

© 2009 me+mi publishing, inc. All rights reserved.
Translation © Gladys Rosa-Mendoza/me+mi publishing, inc.
Printed in China.

REINFORCED LIBRARY EDITION

Library of Congress Cataloging-in-Publication Data

Espluga, Maria.
I, sailor = Yo, marinero / Maria Espluga.
p. cm.
Summary: A young boy who dreams of becoming a sailor embarks on a sea adventure.
ISBN 978-1-931398-53-4 (hardcover)
[1. Sailors—Fiction. 2. Spanish language materials—Bilingual.]
I. Title. II. Title: Yo, marinero.
PZ73.E775 2009
[E]—dc22
2008041182